Visit the Library's On-line Catalog at:
http://www.zionsville.lib.in.us

Call the Library for information on access
if Internet is not available to you.
(317) 873-3149

On-line magazine index with full text at:
http://www.inspire-indiana.net

Book form 2-1

Dear Parent:

Buckle up! You are about to join your child on a very exciting journey. The destination? Independent reading!

Road to Reading will help you and your child get there. The program offers books at five levels, or Miles, that accompany children from their first attempts at reading to successfully reading on their own. Each Mile is paved with engaging stories and delightful artwork.

Getting Started
For children who know the alphabet and are eager to begin reading
• easy words • fun rhythms • big type • picture clues

Reading With Help
For children who recognize some words and sound out others with help
• short sentences • pattern stories • simple plotlines

Reading On Your Own
For children who are ready to read easy stories by themselves
• longer sentences • more complex plotlines • easy dialogue

First Chapter Books
For children who want to take the plunge into chapter books
• bite-size chapters • short paragraphs • full-color art

Chapter Books
For children who are comfortable reading independently
• longer chapters • occasional black-and-white illustrations

There's no need to hurry through the Miles. Road to Reading is designed without age or grade levels. Children can progress at their own speed, developing confidence and pride in their reading ability no matter what their age or grade.

So sit back and enjoy the ride—every Mile of the way!

For Karen Lavut,
who looked at an elephant and saw a dancer
M.K.

To my wife Beth
and my kids, Wolf and Teal
M.M.

Special thanks to Patrick Thomas, Curator,
Department of Mammals,
Wildlife Conservation Society, Bronx, NY.

Library of Congress Cataloging-in-Publication Data
Kulling, Monica.
Elephants : life in the wild / by Monica Kulling ; illustrated by Michael
Maydak.
  p.   cm. — (Road to reading. Mile 3)
Summary: Describes the physical characteristics, habitat, family life, and
eating habits of both African and Asian elephants.
ISBN 0-307-46332-X (GB) — ISBN 0-307-26332-0 (pbk)
1. Elephants—Juvenile literature. [1. Elephants.] I. Maydak, Michael, ill.
II. Title. III. Series.
QL737.P98 K84 2000
599.67—dc21   99-086946

A GOLDEN BOOK • New York
Golden Books Publishing Company, Inc. New York, New York 10106

ISBN: 0-307-26332-0 (pbk)
ISBN: 0-307-46332-X (GB)   A MM

Elephants
Life in the Wild

by Monica Kulling
illustrated by Michael Maydak

It's early morning
on the African plain.
A baby elephant wanders
a few steps from her mother.
In the bushes, a hungry lion watches.

Suddenly, the mother elephant
spreads out her huge ears.
Danger is near!
She lifts her trunk and trumpets loudly.
BLAAARRE!

Soon the ground is shaking

and dust is flying.

Her family is coming!

The lion turns and runs away.
There's no way she'll fight
a herd of angry elephants.

Elephants are the largest
animals on land.
Some weigh up to
15,000 pounds—
as much as a bus!

Because they are so big,
elephants have to eat
almost 400 pounds of food
each day just to survive.
Elephants start eating
before the sun comes up
and eat for twenty hours a day.

Elephants are plant eaters,
or *herbivores*.
They eat grass, leaves,
and tree bark.

They are lucky—
they can reach food
most other animals can't.
When an elephant stands
on its back legs,
it can stretch higher
than a giraffe!

Elephants are able to live in more
than one place, or *habitat*.
Some elephants live on grassy plains
called *savannahs*.
Other elephants live in rain forests.
A few even live in the desert!

There are two kinds, or *species*,
of elephant—African and Asian.

AFRICA

The African elephant
lives in Africa.
Its huge ears are shaped
like a map of Africa.

The Asian elephant lives in India
and other parts of Asia.

INDIA

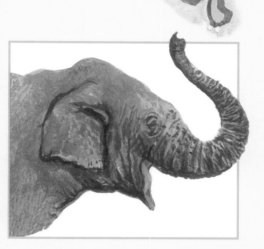

Its ears are smaller—
and they're shaped like
a map of India.

The African elephant has
one bump on top of its head
and a "two-finger" trunk.

The Asian elephant has
two bumps on top of its head
and a "one-finger" trunk.

An elephant's trunk is made of
thousands of muscles.
It is strong but gentle.
It can pull up a whole tree by its roots
or pick a tiny blade of grass.
When it is relaxed,
a trunk can measure eight feet!

The trunk has all kinds of uses.

It is a hand for gathering,

a hose for showering,

and a straw for drinking.

It is even a snorkel for swimming!

An elephant's tusks are almost
as useful as its trunk.
Tusks are long, pointed teeth
made of ivory.
They grow four to seven inches a year.
Most elephants have them,
except for female Asian elephants.

Just as people are
right-handed or left-handed,
elephants use one tusk
more than the other.
One tusk is always
more worn down than its mate.

Elephants use their tusks
to dig for water and tear bark off trees.
Male elephants defend their territory
by fighting other males with their tusks.

The males leave the herd
when they are thirteen years old.
Most of them travel alone.
Some may travel with one or two
other male elephants.

Female elephants live in family groups.

They stay together their whole lives.

The oldest female in the family

is called the *matriarch*.

She is the leader.

She is usually the biggest

and can be over sixty years old.

This baby elephant looks tiny
next to her mother.
But she is really very large.
A baby elephant usually weighs
150 to 250 pounds at birth.
Human babies weigh only
about five to ten pounds.

For the first few days,
the baby elephant walks
under her mother's belly.
She is safest there.

As she grows,

the elephant is looked after

by all the females in the family.

They teach her how to find food and water.

This baby elephant
has a lot to learn.
She doesn't know how
to use her trunk yet.
Sometimes she
trips over it.

Sometimes she sucks
it like a thumb!

It will take five or six days
before she learns to drink
with her trunk.
Until then, she kneels by the water
and drinks with her mouth.

Elephants spray themselves
with water to keep cool.
Elephants cool off
in other ways, too.
Sometimes they flap their ears.
Other times they wallow in mud.
An elephant's skin is over
an inch thick in some places.
The deep wrinkles trap the mud
and keep the elephant cool.

This herd of African elephants
is moving to a new grazing spot.
Elephants walk quietly,
even though they are heavy.
Their weight rests on the ends
of their toes.

Thick pads cushion each step.

You could say that an elephant

walks on its tiptoes!

Suddenly, the matriarch
hears rumbling.
She knows the sound is coming
from another elephant family.

Elephants make this rumbling sound
at the back of their throats.
The rumbling is *infrasonic*—
which means that it is
too low for humans to hear.

A scientist named Katy Payne
recorded elephant rumbles.
She learned that elephants use
this sound to keep in touch.
The sound tells them
that other family groups are near.
That way they know not to eat
in the same place.

Elephants "talk" in other ways, too.
They greet one another
by wrapping their trunks together
or by putting their trunks
in the ears or mouths
of other elephants.

They also send messages with their ears.

The matriarch sticks her ears out

when there is danger.

She flaps her ears to tell her family

when to eat or rest.

Elephants seem almost human.

They live in family groups.

They take care of each other.

Scientists believe that they

have feelings like ours.

They get excited when they meet.

They get sad when a member

of their family dies.

They may even shed tears.

At one time, elephants were
in danger of becoming extinct.
Poachers killed them
for their ivory tusks.

But today, selling ivory is illegal.

Elephants are protected from poachers.

Night falls on the plain.

The herd gathers to sleep.

Some of the elephants

sleep standing up

while some lie down.

Others make pillows

for their heads out of plants.

The elephants will sleep
for only a few hours.
Before sunrise,
they will be on the move again.

04/01